S N O W Y

Berlie Doherty
Illustrated by Keith Bowen

Collins
An Imprint of HarperCollins*Publishers*

For Rachel

First published in Great Britain by
HarperCollins Publishers Ltd in 1992
10 9 8 7 6 5 4 3
First published in Picture Lions in 1993
10 9 8 7 6 5 4
Picture Lions is an imprint of the Children's Division,
part of HarperCollins Publishers Limited,
77-85 Fulham Palace Road, Hammersmith,
London W6 8JB

Text copyright © Berlie Doherty 1992
Illustrations copyright © Keith Bowen 1992
The author and illustrator assert the moral right to be
identified as the author and illustrator of the work.

A CIP catalogue record for this book
is available from the British Library.

ISBN 0 00 193461-9 Hb
ISBN 0 00 664297-7 Pb

Printed in the People's Republic of China

This book is set in Goudy 16/23

Rachel doesn't live in a house.

She lives in a kind of barge called a narrowboat, on a kind
of river called a canal. Her boat is painted yellow and red
and blue. There are castles and roses painted on the side of it,
and on the buckets and kettles on the roof.

At night, when she goes to bed, she can feel the narrowboat rocking gently from side to side. She can hear the slish! slosh! of water against its sides. Everything inside is small and cosy and bright, and she lives there with her mum and dad.

She loves her narrowboat.

It's called Betelgeuse, which is a kind of star, but Rachel calls it Beetle Juice. The best thing about living on a boat, better than the rocking at night, better than the castles and roses, better than the splish! splash! of the water on its sides, is Snowy.

Snowy is the boat horse.

She lives in a stable on the banks of the canal, and her job is to pull Beetle Juice along the water when Rachel's mum and dad take people for rides.

She's as white as a horse of snow. She's taller than Dad. She has long hair like feathers round her hooves. Mum puts a bridle on her, and ropes with coloured bobbins on, and jingling bells, and shining brasses, and under her tail she has a stick called a swingle-tree to hitch the long, long rope to. The other end of the rope is tied to Beetle Juice.

When Mum clicks her tongue and says, "Come on, Snowy," she lowers her head and pulls. Then she plod, plod, plods along the towpath, and her long rope stretches behind her, and Beetle Juice floats along the canal like a painted swan.

"Please, please can I take Snowy to school?" Rachel asked her mum one morning. "Miss Sniff said we can take our pets today."

"Snowy isn't a pet," said Mum. She brushed Rachel's yellow hair as if she was brushing Snowy's tail. "She has to work for a living, like me and Dad and Miss Smith."

She tied Rachel's hair in plaits, and put coloured ribbons on.

"But can't she have a day off, just today?" Rachel made her eyes round and big to show how much she wanted to take Snowy to school, but Mum wasn't looking.

"No," said Mum. "Snowy has to work today."

Rachel cried all the way to school, but Mum didn't change her mind.

And that day Benny brought a grey rabbit that shivered like the grass in the wind. Simon brought a fish with raggedy fins that floated in its bowl like a golden shirt on a washing line. Yasmine brought a stick insect that pretended to be just an old twig. Will wobbled his front tooth with his tongue.

"Where's your pet?" he asked Rachel.

Rachel put her finger through the button hole in her cardigan.

"She's gone to work," she said.

They all laughed so much that some of them started coughing.

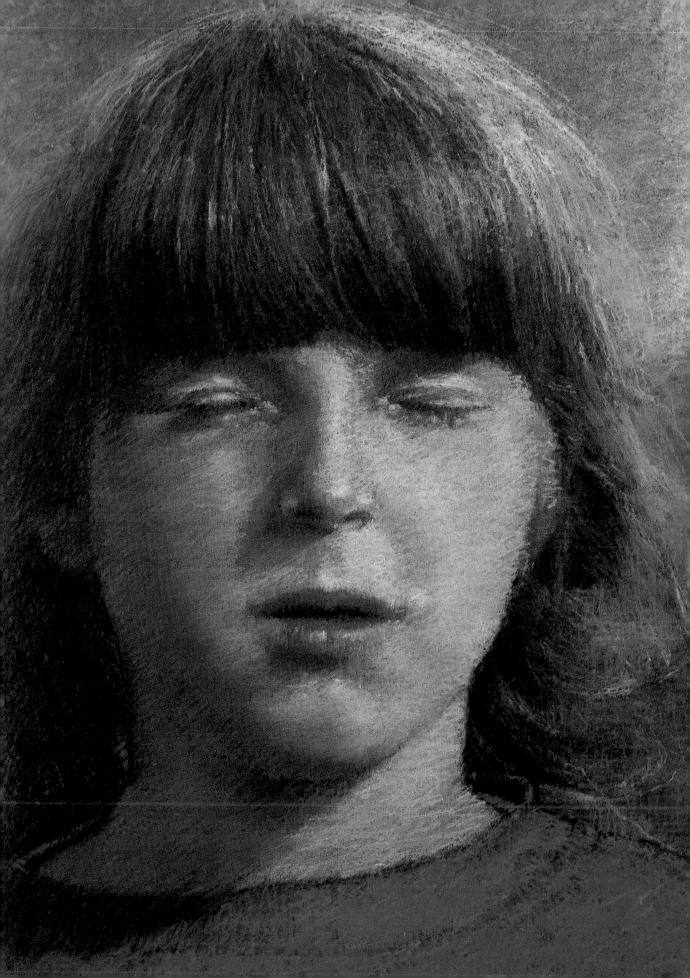

Will wobbled his tooth again. His tongue squashed in
and out round it. "What's she like?"

Rachel closed her eyes. "She's as big as a mountain,"
she said. "And she's got bells and ribbons and a swingle-tree.
And she smells like a haystack."

Everybody laughed again. Rachel kept her eyes closed.
"And she's got feathers round her feet," she said.

"I'd rather have my stick insect," said Yasmine.

Rachel cried.

That evening Miss Smith came to the canal and sat on the grass with Mum. Dad made some tea in the little kitchen that was called a galley. He whistled his favourite tune and toasted some teacakes and put yellow runny butter on them, and they sat in the sun and ate them.

There were lots of people sitting on the grass outside their narrowboats. Some of them were playing banjoes and mouth organs, and some of them were gossiping about each other, and some of them were just enjoying the sunshine.

But Rachel went into the dark stable that smelt of haystacks and put her arms round one of Snowy's front legs. She rested her head against her soft white side, and cried.

Next afternoon, at school, Miss Smith told the class that they weren't going to have a story that day. They all folded their arms and looked tidy and promised to be good if they could have a story, but Miss Smith laughed and said they were going to have something even better than a story.

She took them outside, and Will's mum and Benny's dad and Mrs Lacy the dinner lady all joined them, all smiling their heads off and full of secrets.

"Are we going for a walk, Miss Sniff?" Rachel asked.

Miss Smith held her hand and told her she could help to lead the way. And the amazing thing was that their walk took them all the way to Rachel's canal, and right up to where Beetle Juice was moored.

"This is where Rachel lives," said Miss Smith.

Everybody loved Beetle Juice. "It's got flowers painted on it!" they shouted.

Rachel pulled up her socks and folded her arms and smiled.
Then she heard the most wonderful sound in the world.

It was Snowy, coming out of the stable that smelt of haystacks.

It was Snowy, with her white hairs like feathers round her hooves, and her bells jingling, and her ropes and coloured bobbins creaking, and all her brasses shining in the sun. Everybody ran to her and gazed up at her with their mouths open.

"Isn't she beautiful!" they said. "Doesn't she smell lovely!"
Will wobbled his tooth. "I wish she was mine," he sighed.
Mum said, "Come on, Snowy. You've got work to do."
She fixed the swingle-tree behind Snowy's tail, and hitched
the tow rope to it.

"All on board!" Dad shouted. He and Miss Smith lifted
the children on to the narrowboat, and Will's mum and
Ben's dad and Mrs Lacy the dinner lady climbed on too,
smiling their heads off.

Mum clicked her tongue. "Come on, Snowy," she said.

Snowy lowered her head and began to move forward, plod,
plod, plod. Mum smiled down at Rachel and held her hand
tight and warm. She put her other hand on Snowy's rope
and they walked along the towpath behind her.

The rope stretched out. Beetle Juice, with all
Rachel's friends on board, began to glide along
the canal, slow and quiet and proud, just like a
painted swan.